THE CHRISTMAS DARE

A BWWM Holiday Romance

A LANGDALE CHRISTMAS
BOOK V

PEYTON BANKS

"Love isn't something you find. Love is something that finds you."

— —LORETTA YOUNG

BLURB

He was supposed to be a holiday fling—not her daily temptation.

June Young had a Christmas tradition—hot cocoa, jammies, and no drama! But when her best friend dares her to have a one-night stand, she decides—for once—to throw caution to the wind.

One night. One scorching-hot stranger. No rules. No regrets.

Mason was tall, sinfully sexy, and knew exactly how to make a woman forget her name. Their chemistry was explosive, their night together unforgettable. June thought she'd leave him in the past, tucked away like a naughty holiday secret.

Until she walked into her brand-new job... and met her new boss—him.

Now every heated glance across the office, every accidental touch, and every memory of what his hands—and mouth—can do drove her insane. And Mason? He's not backing down. He wants more than one night, and he's ready to play dirty to get it.

Workplace rules are about to be broken, small-town tongues are bound to wag, and June's carefully controlled world is about to go up in a blaze of holiday heat.

The Christmas Dare is a steamy BWWM holiday romance that will leave you hot under the mistletoe. This short novella is reserved for mature readers only.

The Little Pint glowed like Christmas itself had come to life within its walls. Every inch of the small-town bar was dressed for the holiday with garlands draped across the long oak bar, twinkle lights wrapped around the ceiling beams, and a massive tree decked out in the corner with gold and red ornaments. Even the scent of Christmas was in the air along with the aroma of delicious bar food.

"I'm so glad you came out," Tanika shouted over the music.

June Young smiled and lifted her drink for a sip. At first, she hadn't wanted to come out, but she knew if she didn't, her bestie would never let her hear the end of it. The jukebox in the corner alternated between classic rock and Christmas hits, and right now Mariah Carey was belting out her annual mantra over the chatter of folks and the clink of glasses.

"Like I had a choice," June replied.

Tanika laughed and elbowed her.

"You sure didn't. You need to get out more. I didn't beg you to move here for nothing," Tanika said.

Her friend didn't truly have to beg her to move to Langdale, Illinois. June had been open to moving anywhere she found a good job that wasn't too far from her family.

She glanced around and smiled. Some locals had donned Santa hats, and someone had strung a line of mistletoe above the dartboard near the pool tables. That line of mistletoe could be a little risky, seeing how much beer had been served tonight.

Behind the bar, glass shelves reflected the soft glow of colored light, and the faint scent of cinnamon whisky and spiced cider hung in the air. A football game played on the mounted television above the bar. The sound was low with subtitles while a digital fireplace crackled on another screen near the door, adding a bit of festive charm. Between the two, June preferred the fireplace. That was what she wished she could have right now.

It was the holidays, and Tanika loved to hang out, but June was not really a bar-scene person. She'd prefer to be snuggled up in front of a fireplace this time of year with her favorite thick blanket, a nice cup of hot cocoa, and a good book.

But, she loved Tanika dearly, so here she was.

She really couldn't complain. She was having fun. It was two weeks before Christmas, and the town of Langdale had fully surrendered to the holiday spirit. The sidewalks were lined with wreaths, outside smelled faintly of pine, and inside the Little Pint, laughter mingled with the hum of Christmas cheer.

Maybe this was what June needed—a distraction from the loneliness the holidays could bring about. She turned to Tanika and gave her a nudge.

"Thank you," June said.

"For what?" Tanika arched an eyebrow.

"For dragging me out the house even though I had big plans," June teased.

"Oh, please. Knowing you, you would have been dressed in some big fluffy robe with your bonnet on, rotting away on the couch." Tanika snorted.

June gasped and pretended to clutch her invisible pearls. Tanika certainly knew her well.

"Well, I'll have you know, I don't own a big fluffy robe. It's cotton," she muttered.

Tanika threw her head back and burst out laughing. June rolled her eyes and joined her. Was she that bad? She reached for her drink again and finished it off.

"Don't hate being a couch potato on the weekends. You might want to try it sometime."

"And that's why I love you." Tanika chuckled.

The two of them had met their freshman year at Illinois State University. June had been an accounting major while Tanika had been a business major. They had been matched as roommates and best friends ever since.

"Whatever," June grumbled. She motioned to their drinks. They had only had one round. Not that she had to drink much to start feeling good, but they could do with a refill and something to eat. "I need some food. You can't get me all liquored up and no food. You know what will happen if I don't get something to counterbalance all of this alcohol."

"I gotcha, boo," Tanika said. She stood and waved down the bartender. "Everything here is good. I would recommend their wings or their cheese curds or their spinach dip or their fried mac and cheese balls...you know what, you can't go wrong with any of their dishes."

June laughed at her. If she said everything on the menu was good, then she trusted her. They were both foodies and loved to cook and try out new recipes. In college when they'd had extra money, they'd gone around town trying out all of the local restaurants and posted reviews online like they were true food critics. That memory brought another smile to June's lips.

"Hey, ladies. Ready for another round?" Devin, the bartender, slid in front of them.

He was nice-looking with a wide grin. He didn't do much for June, but the ladies around the bar were certainly trying to catch his attention.

"Dev, we're looking for something to eat and another round of drinks. You want the same drink?" Tanika turned to June who nodded.

She was going to play it safe with her favorite drink when she did go out. Cranberry and vodka. Simple and good. No need to try anything else. Half of the drinks on the menu, she didn't know what they were. Nope, she was going to stick with what she knew, and what she knew was she liked cranberry juice and she liked vodka.

"What about food?"

"You choose. I trust you," June said.

Tanika placed their order. She frequented the Little Pint enough that June was sure she knew what they'd both like from the menu. June glanced around at the bar and took in the locals having a great time. Couples cozied up on the dance floor, some sitting together, while plenty of people crowded around the pool tables. A slight twinge entered her chest as she took in a couple sharing an intimate moment. She had been single for a while. Her heart was a little bruised from her last relationship. She had figured it would have amounted to a ring. But apparently, he'd had other things on his mind—like two other women. How she hadn't recognized the signs, she didn't know. She'd worked a lot and thought he had, too.

Five years should have ended with them becoming engaged and planning a future. She was thirty-six years old and she was not getting any younger. She was not afraid to admit she wanted a husband, a few kids who would grow up in a loving home, but right now, she was going to focus on herself and her new job.

"So, Miss Ma'am." Tanika faced her after she'd finished ordering.

June eyed her. The woman was up to something. The glint in her eye was a dead giveaway, and it had nothing to do with the one drink they had already consumed.

"What is it?" June asked dryly.

Tanika giggled and tucked her dark hair behind her ear. "We need to have fun."

"Isn't that why we are here? I'm having fun." June tilted her head to the side to study her. Oh, Tanika Fisher was up to something all right.

"I mean, we should be out here living life," Tanika gushed.

"I am. I start a new job on Monday. I have a new home that is nice—"

"That is all boring adulting stuff. I mean fun-fun." Tanika winked at her.

June sighed and shook her head. "You are going to have to explain what fun-fun means."

"Well, Miss Goody Two-Shoes, you have been on Santa's nice list for far too long. Time to get naughty for once." Tanika scooted her chair closer to June's.

The bar was starting to get a little crowded. June was starting to regret taking a seat at the counter and not finding a table.

"I think I like it on the nice list," June murmured.

"Oh, please. That is boring. How brave do you feel tonight?"

Tanika propped her elbow on the counter and rested her chin in her palm. She wiggled her eyebrows, and that just confirmed what June was suspecting.

June didn't know how to answer. She knew her friend well, and Tanika was way more spontaneous than June was. But June was curious as to what she was hinting at.

"What are you thinking?" June sighed. She might as well ask since Tanika was trying to be mysterious with whatever she was concocting in that brain of hers.

"Let's play a game. Wanna play Dare?"

"Don't you mean Truth or Dare?" June asked for clarification.

Devin returned with their drinks and a bowl of fried cheese curds. He promised the rest of the order should be out soon. June popped one of the curds in her mouth. It was amazing. She chewed and waited for Tanika to respond.

"Well, the truth part would be no fun. We practically know everything about each other, and if we don't then we need to reevaluate this friendship," Tanika teased.

"I'm sure there is something we don't know about each other," June shot back. She was a bit nervous about just a game of Dare.

"Oh, come on, Junie! Let your hair

down. Have fun for once in your life," Tanika groaned. She popped another cheese curd in her mouth. "What's the harm?"

June reached for her drink to buy herself some more time. She took a sip and winced. Devin was trying to make sure all of his patrons either tipped well or fell on their ass. June tasted a hint of cranberry, but her drink was mainly all vodka.

"Stop stalling!" Tanika exclaimed.

"Okay, fine. I'm probably going to regret this," June muttered.

"Oh, please. Have I ever led you wrong before?"

Tanika's eyes grew wide, and she tried to give off an innocent look, but June read right through the bullshit. June glared at her, and Tanika fell into a fit of laughter.

"Okay, okay. One time. We made our way home, though."

One summer they had gone camping. Which was not something June did, but Tanika had an idea to go camping at a state park in Wyoming. They'd gone on a hike and got lost. Ended up three miles away from their campsite while it was getting dark. Lucky for them, park rangers had found them and guided them back to where they were supposed to be.

"I will play your game." June sighed. She reached for another curd and popped it in her mouth. The taste exploded on her tongue, and she couldn't hold back a groan.

"You ladies look as if you are having way too much fun over here," a deep baritone voice sounded behind them.

June and Tanika spun around in their seats.

"Mason. How are you?" Tanika asked.

June was rendered speechless. Mason was tall, broad-shouldered, with dark-blond hair that fell forward on his forehead. He combed it back, and June's heart stuttered. He had a light beard which was one thing that she loved. She inhaled slightly and caught the scent of his cologne. She didn't know what it was, but it definitely had her wanting to get closer to him so she could breathe it in more.

But the simple fact she had to tilt her head back to look up at him had the butterflies in her stomach awakening. June had some height to her. She stood five feet nine without heels. Most men she'd dated in the past hated when she'd thrown them on because she'd either be the same height as them or taller. Not that she wore killer heels, but a good three- to four-inch was her go-to.

Tall women did something to a man's ego who may not be blessed with height himself.

"I'm good," he said.

His gaze switched to June and swept over her in the same way she had been eyeing him. The heat that appeared in his eyes had her squeezing her legs together.

"Who do we have here?" he asked.

"Oh, I'm sorry. Where are my manners? Mason, this is my friend, June. June, this is Mason," Tanika said.

"It's nice to meet you." Mason switched his longneck to the other hand and wiped his palm on his jeans before offering a hand to her.

June blinked and stared at the larger hand before slipping hers into his.

"Likewise," June said.

She swallowed hard to get rid of the lump that had formed in her throat. The feeling of his big hand engulfing hers sent those butterflies into overdrive. When he pulled back from her, she almost protested. The callused feeling of his palm would feel so damn good running along her inner thighs. Her breath caught in her throat at the thought. She glanced up at him again and took in the beard.

Hell, that would feel good running over her soft skin, too. She had to pull her thoughts out of the gutter.

"Hey, Devin. Put their food on my tab," Mason called out to him.

"Sure thing, man," Devin shouted back.

"You don't have to do that," Tanika said.

"Don't worry about it. Consider it an early Christmas gift," he said.

"Well, thank you," June said. Her heart stuttered once again at his crooked grin. She didn't know what was happening, but this man certainly did something to her. Her body was going haywire the longer he remained next to her.

"You just move here? I don't think we've met before," he murmured. He stepped closer to her as someone was trying to scoot by behind him. The Little Pint was obviously a popular spot. The crowd was growing thicker.

"Do you know everyone in Langdale?" she asked playfully. She reached for her glass so she would have something in her hands and not reach for him. She looked over it as she sipped.

"Almost." He chuckled.

"Mason owns a business here. Everyone knows Mason and his family." Tanika grinned. Her gaze moved between Mason and June. The glint that was in her eyes suddenly grew brighter.

"Well, apparently, June doesn't know me, so I'd say not everyone." He brought the bottle to his lips and took a swig.

June's gaze swept back down him to his chest that was covered under a thick dark sweater. It didn't take much to see the man was in top physical shape. She didn't know a business owner could look this good. All the ones she had worked for before or knew were a little soggy around the middle.

The music shifted to one of June's favorite Christmas songs. The beginning of 'Let it Snow' by Boyz II Men came on. June immediately glanced over at the dance floor.

Other couples had made their way and swayed along to the song.

"I love this song." She sighed.

"Mason will take you out there," Tanika announced.

June's head flew back around. Was her friend insane? The wide grin on Tanika's face proved it. The woman knew what she was doing, and it was apparent that the dare had been issued.

"Won't you, Mason?"

"Sure, why not." He drained the rest of his beer and set the empty bottle on the counter. He held out his hand to June.

"You don't have to."

June shook her head, but Mason and Tanika weren't listening to her.

He grinned and tugged her by the hand down from her chair. "I don't bite."

His deep chuckle had her core clenching. He led her through the throng of people. She tried to look over her shoulder at her friend, but the sight of Tanika was swallowed up by the crowd. They ended up on the floor right in the center. Mason pulled her close to him. They fit together perfectly.

He was tall enough that she had to tilt her head back to look at him.

"I'm sorry Tanika made you do this," she said.

He led her in a gentle sway of the music. She had to admit the man had rhythm. He held her close so their bodies molded together. Any other time she would have put space between herself and a man she'd just met, but for some reason she leaned into him. The hardness of his body could be felt underneath the sweater. He felt like how she'd imagined he would, and she inhaled sharply.

Mistake.

The scent of his cologne accosted her. She didn't know what it was, but she went ahead and tossed caution to the wind and leaned in and breathed deeply.

"No one can make me do anything." His deep voice rumbled in his chest.

His hand settled at the curve of her back. She wore a long tunic sweater, leggings, and comfy boots. With the amount of snow that had fallen, she had chosen her practical boots in this weather. She'd heard Langdale was known for crazy amounts of snow, and so far, the town hadn't let her down.

"Besides, a beautiful woman wanting to dance, I couldn't pass up the opportunity."

"Well, thank you anyway," she murmured.

She lifted her head from his shoulder and met his eyes again. They were a warm brown with hints of gold flecks. An electric current rippled through her. This man was definitely doing something to her. She ran her hand along his shoulder to rest at the nape of his neck.

"I'm just glad you don't have two left feet."

He barked a laugh and twirled her around slowly.

"I've done this before," he said by her ear.

It was then the large bulge pressed on her stomach. She whimpered, and all the dirty thoughts and fantasies she'd pushed out of her mind came flooding back. Her body automatically rubbed against him. He lifted his head, and his hooded eyes connected with hers.

Oh, the dare hadn't been the dance. The

dare had been the man himself. Tanika wouldn't go so far as to dare her to go home with a man for a one-night stand.

Or would she?

The song came to an end, and a fast-paced rock song from the eighties came on. They broke apart and stared at each other for a moment.

"I better get back to Tanika," she breathed.

He jerked his head in a nod. She began making her way through the crowd. She wasn't sure how his hand ended up in hers and their fingers entwined. She arrived back at the bar with Mason right behind her. Tanika turned from chatting with a guy next to her. The woman's grin split from one ear to another.

"Have fun?" she asked.

Mason leaned on the bar and tried to flag Devin down.

"Um, yeah," June said. Her heart hadn't gone back to normal yet. It was pounding away like a runaway train. She glanced over at Mason who struck up a conversation with the guy next to him about the game on the screen.

"So, back to our game." Tanika leaned into June, placing her lips near June's ear. "I dare you to go home with Mason. Tonight."

June was right. That was her friend's dare. She bit her lip and contemplated. Could she do this? Could she go home with a man she'd only just met? Tanika knew him, so that had to amount to something, right? She glanced back at Tanika who winked at her.

"Tanika..." she said.

The woman knew June wasn't that type of girl. One-night stands had never been her thing before. She'd always been safe with dating a guy for at least a few weeks before sliding between the sheets with him.

"What do you have to lose? Have fun. You're here for a new start. Why not start with him?" Tanika teased.

June glanced over at Mason. The memory of his hands on her clothed body came to mind. Her breath caught in her throat at the thought of those same hands on her naked skin.

What the hell. A woman only lived once, right?

Mind made up, and filled with determination, June tapped Mason on the shoulder. He turned to her and ducked down to where her mouth was next to his ear since the crowd watching the game decided to go wild at that exact moment.

"What's up, pretty little lady?"

"Do you want to get out of here and maybe go back to your place?"

❧ 2 ❧

The cold night air hit him square in the chest the moment he stepped outside. It was bitter, sharp, but clean with the faint edge of more incoming snow. He tugged his jacket tighter while his boots crunched on the snow as they crossed the lot. He glanced down at her.

June.

She was all soft curves with a smile that had taken his breath away. Her wool hat was pulled down over her hair, and a few flakes of snow stuck to the dark material. She looked up at him and smiled. Her eyes went wide just as she slipped. He quickly reached out and held her up.

"Be careful there, Junie B. We wouldn't

want you falling now, would we?" He grinned. He helped straighten her up and took her by the hand.

"That's all I would have needed." She rolled her eyes with her smile widening.

"I mean, if you wanted to be in my arms now, you could have just said so," he teased.

"Oh, please," she giggled.

She playfully pushed at him, but he held her tight to him, and they continued the trek to his truck. He was glad he had automatic start and had triggered the vehicle to turn on while they had grabbed their coats. It should be nice and toasty once they got in.

"Is your car here?" he asked.

"No, Tanika and I called for an Uber. We didn't want to risk driving in this weather, plus we had planned to have a few drinks." A gust of wind blew, causing June to move closer to him.

He tried to shield her with his body as much as he could.

"That was responsible of you," he said.

They arrived at his truck. The snow on the windshield was already thawing out.

"Oh God. You sound like my mother," she said.

He positioned her near the truck so he could open the door for her.

"I do? That's not what I'm going for at all." He chuckled.

He moved closer to her. She tilted her head back so her eyes could meet his. He saw she was still weighing up her decision about asking him to take her home. His gaze dropped down to her plump lips, and he immediately had to look away.

The fantasy of them wrapped around his cock had him hardening.

"Do I even want to know what you're aiming for?" She arched an eyebrow at him.

He grinned and opened the door. He chose to ignore her question. He wasn't sure she would be ready to hear what he was really thinking.

"Hop in, sweetheart," he murmured.

She slipped her hand back in his and climbed into the truck, and for one heartbeat, Mason had to admit he felt more than a spark of an attraction to this woman. He assisted her with putting on her safety belt before he shut the door. He exhaled, rounding the hood of the vehicle to the driver's door. He pulled his gloves out of his pocket and threw them on and tried to brush the rest of the snow off the windshield.

Get it together, man.

June looking at him with those big brown eyes, all he could think about was what she would taste like if he kissed her.

Or what she'd look like reaching her climax riding his cock.

Fuck.

"Still cold?" He climbed in and tossed his gloves in the back seat. He combed the snow from his hair. He had to stop acting like he was some teenage boy with his first crush.

"Not really." She glanced at him with her flushed brown cheeks while her voice had a slight tremor to it.

The cab was slightly warmer than outside. The temperature had certainly dropped since he'd first arrived at the Little Pint. He cranked the heat higher.

"Good. I'd hate to think I wasn't doing my job," he said.

Her lips twitched where she tried to

hide her smile. He threw the engine into drive and pulled out of the spot. Soft rock played low on the radio.

"And what job is that?" That perfectly sculpted eyebrow of hers rose.

He barked a hefty laugh and drove the truck out onto the snow-covered road.

"Taking care of you, Junie girl." He tossed her a wink before turning his attention back to the road.

The truck heater kicked on, causing the windows to fog up. The snow fell even harder with the flakes blurring against the windshield. June sat quietly beside him, her perfume filling the cab. It was something sweet and made his body react to her.

"So, do you live close by?" June asked.

"Close enough." He tried to keep the truck at a steady, easy pace so he didn't drive them off into a ditch in the snow. He tightened his grip on the steering wheel. He glanced back over at her. "Where are you from?"

"Peoria. I moved here for a job."

"Really? That's pretty cool. I grew up here. Left for college then came back home," he said.

"But now I'm looking at all this snow, and it has me second-guessing that decision. How do people survive in all this?" A nervous chuckle escaped her as she stared out the window.

"We make it. Mother Nature just likes to show off. You'll survive," Mason said. He was used to the weather in Langdale. Every year they had at least one or two big snowstorms that shut their small town down. It wouldn't be Langdale without them.

Silence settled between them. Not awkward but charged. Electricity hummed in the air. The cab was suddenly hot and stuffy. He reached over and lowered the heat. He could feel her peeking his way every so often, and each time she did, it felt like the temperature ticked up another degree.

Mason reached up and unzipped his coat a little. His body was on edge with the thought of taking this sexy woman home. He'd seen the looks of some of the other guys as they'd made their way out. Any chances they had hoped to have with her were gone. She had chosen him. He'd only decided to stop by for a few drinks since he'd just got back into town.

He'd had a meeting with the governor to do a presentation for bidding on a couple of projects that were put out for small businesses. He'd been in and out of town for the past two weeks and hadn't even really been around the office. He already dreaded Monday where he was sure his office manager, Blair, would have plenty of items lined up and waiting for him.

So, to help start his weekend, he'd decided to stop by the Little Pint for some beers and to watch the game. Never in his wildest dreams did he see himself leaving with a woman like June. It had been a while since he'd had a one-night stand, but in all of his forty-two years, he'd never had a woman make the first move and ask to go home with him.

He blinked and focused on the road. He'd made this trip hundreds of times, and tonight, it seemed to take longer.

They veered onto his street, the truck's headlights cutting through the trees heavy with snow. His porch light glowed as they arrived. He drove up the driveway and parked. He killed the engine and turned to her. She looked up at him with those big brown eyes.

"We made it." He cleared his throat. His voice came out much rougher than he meant it to be.

"Yeah, we did. Was there any doubt we wouldn't?" A twinkle glittered in her eye.

"Junie B, you are going to see that you can trust me to keep you safe." He meant that. He could see the nervousness in her eyes. He had a feeling that Junie didn't go around asking men to take her home. Something in his chest tightened at the thought that she was stepping out of her comfort zone. He'd make sure she wouldn't regret this decision. She may be having second thoughts of the snow and Langdale, but he didn't want there to be any doubt about her spending the night with him.

"I hope so," she whispered. Her gaze darted down to his mouth, then back to his eyes.

He leaned closer to her. June's breath hitched. That was all it took.

"Are you sure, Junie? I can take you home if you want." He wanted to ensure she was certain on what they were about to embark on.

For a second, neither of them moved. The air between them pulsed with heat.

Then she smiled, and Mason knew he was done for.

"Invite me in, Mason."

THE DOOR CLOSED BEHIND HER WITH A click that echoed through the quiet. The warmth of the home hit her first. She unzipped her coat and stomped the snow from her boots. They both removed their coats and footwear. The cold outside had quickly tried to seep into her as they had rushed into the house. Mason's home was softly lit, with lamplight spilling across the dark hardwood floors. The faint hint of cedar and pine wrapped around her.

"I'll take your coat," Mason said.

She handed it to him while she moved her boots over to where his sat. She reached up and tucked her hair behind her ear. He shut the closet and spun back to her. For a moment, neither of them spoke. The only sound was the pounding of her heart beating, wild and erratic.

Then he reached for her.

Mason stood before her, making her tilt her head back to return his heated gaze. His hand brushed a lock of her hair from her face. His fingertips grazed her cheeks. Her breath caught at his touch. His eyes were dark and searching, as if to ask once more the question she had already answered.

"Mason..." Her voice was barely audible.

He didn't answer but waited for her to continue. That alone sped up her heart rate even more. The heat between them should have been enough to ignite a fire right where they stood. She stepped forward until her chest brushed his and rested a palm above his heart.

"Just one night. No strings."

His jaw tightened for a second. She almost thought he would be changing his mind. She studied him. Was this new for him, too? Was he hoping for more after tonight? She couldn't promise anything right now. She had a new job she wanted to focus on that she was starting on Monday. That was where her priority should be.

She'd take this night and then move on.

Or could she?

"One night," he said.

Then he kissed her. The move sent her falling back against the wall behind her. A moan immediately erupted from her. The kiss wasn't soft and docile. It was hungry, deep and possessive. It was the kind of kiss that forced her to forget the cold outside, her name, and everything else except the heat combusting between them. His hands slid down to her hips, drawing their lower bodies together.

Somewhere between kisses he had lifted her from the floor with her legs wrapped around his waist. He walked her through the living room, past the glow of the Christmas tree in the corner, down a short hallway to a shadowed doorway.

He raised his head and reached for the door. She held on as he walked into his bedroom. A lamp on the nightstand was on, basking the room in a creamy hue. He moved them over to the bed and paused. She slid down his body to stand in front of him. The look in his eyes was something dangerous. It made her want to take back her request of only one night. Maybe that had been a mistake. His hands came to rest on the edge of her tunic, and he tugged it over her head.

The pure hunger in his eyes at the sight of her gave her confidence. She reached behind her and unhooked her bra. It fell away onto the floor and joined her top. The second his hands brushed her bare skin, she forgot about all else.

❦ 3 ❦

"What do you mean, you just left?" Tanika was in a full fit of giggles this morning.

June rolled her eyes at her friend enjoying the unfortunate ending of her night with Mason.

"You know I don't do things like this. I didn't know what else to do. I woke up, snuck in the bathroom, got dressed, called for a ride, and then I tried to slip out, but he woke up."

"And what did he say?"

"He asked me for my number," June admitted. She maneuvered her car through the slight traffic. It was bright and early Monday morning, and she didn't want to be late for her new job. First impressions meant a lot to her, so she was going to make sure she was on time today. She blew out a deep breath as the memory of Saturday morning came forward. She had to admit, she had panicked when Mason had asked for her number.

The night with him—unbelievable. A shiver rippled down her spine at the memory of it. That man had drawn orgasms out of her like no other before him. From his tongue to the way his cock had stretched her—

She blinked and had to focus on the road. She hit the brakes and narrowly missed bumping the car in front of her which had stopped at a red light.

That man was certainly dangerous.

"What did you say? You did give it to him, right?" Tanika's voice broke through her thoughts.

June grimaced.

"Well, I sort of told him if it's meant to be maybe we'll run into each other," she admitted.

It had been a lousy way to say no, but it was all she could think of. She didn't know why she had let Tanika talk her into going home with Mason.

Well, not that she was going to complain about what had gone on between the two of them. Her voice was still sort of hoarse from all the screaming she'd done.

"What!" Tanika screeched. "Girl, you did not."

"I did," June replied dryly. She eyed the coffee shop on the corner and decided she'd stop and get a cup of coffee before work. She had plenty of time before she had to report to the office. Once the light switched to green, she made her way over to the Java Hut and found a parking spot.

"Girl, you do realize that—"

"Hey, I got to go. I need to grab some coffee." June cut her off. If she let her, Tanika would keep going on and on about her first one-night stand when all June wanted to do was put it behind her. She would probably never see Mason again. Langdale was a small town, but it wasn't that damn small where they'd run into each other again so soon.

Yes, she'd put her magical night behind her.

She had a new career to focus on, and daydreaming about riding Mason's big cock was not going to pay her bills.

"But—"

"I'll talk to you later. I'll call you after work when I get home. I promise," June said.

"You better!"

June disconnected the call before Tanika could get another word in. She smiled and shook her head as she reached for her purse. She hopped out and went inside the Java Hut. She'd heard good things about this place. It didn't take her long at all to grab the tallest coffee they had and a warm cinnamon crunch muffin. It looked too good to pass up. She should be eating something healthier for breakfast, but her nerves were getting the best of her, and she had a weakness for sweets.

She hopped back into her car and continued on her way. Midwest Contractors was located in the heart of Downtown Langdale which wasn't much farther way from the coffee shop. June pulled into the parking lot and found a spot. She killed the engine and gazed at the building.

"You're going to do fine," she breathed. She reached for her coffee and took a sip. It was quite delightful, and she understood what all the rage was about. She glanced at the time and figured she'd better go in now. She was still about half an hour early. She would just explain her excitement.

She grabbed her things and headed inside the festive-looking building. On the outside, fake Christmas trees had been decked out with red, white, and silver ornaments. She smiled at the thought that went into turning the outside of the building into a Christmas display. That alone let her know this company was the right fit.

She'd done her research, and the company had a great reputation for being trustworthy, was financially stable, was innovative, and had a positive online presence. The company was also known to be a fair employer with competitive wages and benefits and offered flexibility with her schedule. All of the things she looked for in an employer. There wasn't much known about the current CEO, Reuben Reynolds, which in a way was fine with her. It wasn't like she was in a big city dealing with a billion-dollar corporation.

She had a feeling she would do well at Midwest Contractors.

June held her head high and crossed the threshold of the entrance. The scent of pine and cinnamon greeted her the moment she closed the door behind her. The lobby was small but inviting and dressed up in its holiday best. A tall Christmas tree stood proudly in the corner, draped with red and white ribbons, tiny hard-hat ornaments, and twinkling lights. Garlands wrapped around the front desk, dotted with little bows and construction-themed ornaments—mini hammers, measuring tapes, and glittery bulldozers.

A cheerful woman dressed in a festive red sweater sat behind the desk typing away on her computer. She glanced up and offered June a warm smile.

"Morning. Can I help you?"

"Good morning. My name is June Young. Today's my—"

"Ah, yes! Blair told me you would be starting today." The young woman laughed.

She stood and offered her hand to June. "My name is Justina. Welcome!"

"Thank you." June returned her smile and handshake. A warm feeling coursed through her. Yes, this was going to be an amazing start to her new future. She stepped back and hefted up her bag on her shoulder. She had brought a few things from home to decorate her office.

"Let me call Blair and get her down here for you." Justina plopped back down in her seat and reached for the phone.

June took the opportunity to walk over to the Christmas tree. Each of the ornaments had a name on them. She assumed they were employees. She smiled, feeling that warming sensation inside her again. One look at the outside of the building, and the lobby gave her the sense the employees took pride in their company. That meant a lot for a newbie.

"Hey, June. She's on her way down now."

June spun on her heels and smiled. "Thank you."

"All settled in?" Blair appeared in the doorway.

It had been a busy day so far. Blair had given June a quick crash course in the daily workings of the company, along with taking her around to meet the office crew. She would eventually meet some of the guys who worked out in the field. Blair had even given her a rundown of the notes the last bookkeeper had left for her, before giving her a chance to set up her office.

June appreciated everything the woman had done for her so far. She was sure she'd have questions for days until she got into the swing of things. There were already piles of work she needed to tackle, but she took a moment to get her office decorated with all of the items she'd brought from home.

"I think so," June said. She was proud of herself. She'd gone the last few hours without one thought of Mason.

Dammit.

She'd just thought about him. Well, at least she'd gone a few hours this time. The longest before this had been twenty minutes. The weekend had been so hard. She couldn't stop thinking about that damn man and his magical tongue and thick cock.

"Good. I know you didn't get to meet the boss during interviews, but he's finally back in the office, so I figured I'd take you up to his office and introduce you." Blair pushed the door open farther.

"Please do. I would love to meet Mr. Reynolds now." June stood from her chair and grabbed her sweater. She'd learned the hallways tended to be a little chilly. She had brought a small space heater because she tended to be a cold baby and liked to keep her office a little warmer than normal. She hurried over to Blair while sliding her sweater onto her shoulders.

"He's been in and out of town trying to secure this big contract with the state," Blair explained as they walked down the hallway.

"That's impressive," June replied.

State contracts meant big bucks would be coming through. Lucky for Midwest Contractors, she had plenty of experience dealing with the state with her last job. This would be a breeze for her. She even still had contacts in the governor's office that she could reach out to.

"He's been working like a maniac lately. I'm sure he'll apologize for not contacting you sooner," Blair said.

She went into more detail about the projects Mr. Reynolds was trying to secure. One for repairing a few bridges and highways and another one for building a nature center right outside Langdale that could bring in tourist dollars. June was impressed with the information.

Blair guided her up the stairs to the third level. There were conference rooms and a few other offices located up here. June remembered interviewing with Blair in her office on this level.

"Fingers crossed we get them. It would mean a lot of money for the company and Langdale."

"I'll cross my fingers and toes." June chuckled. She wasn't sure why, but her stomach felt funny. She hoped it wasn't that coffee and muffin she'd eaten. Maybe it was her nerves. She had been nervous about meeting everyone, but that had gone away. So far, they had all been wonderful and welcoming.

But this was the boss. She'd hadn't

gotten the chance to speak with him or even interview with him. Apparently, he trusted Blair's decision to hire her. She blew out a deep breath as they came to the double doors at the end of the hall.

"I believe he should be free. This man does nothing but work." Blair sighed. She rapped on the door a few times.

A muffled voice could be heard on the other side. June straightened to her full height, even though her stomach chose that moment to do a flip.

Blair smiled at her and must have seen her nervousness. "You'll be fine. Mason wouldn't hurt a fly."

June stumbled back a step or two. Who? It couldn't be. It had to be a coincidence. Mason was a pretty common name. Wasn't it? Blair entered the office first with June right behind her.

"Hey, Mason. I wanted to introduce you to our new accountant. The one I had been telling you about," Blair said.

June stood in the doorway and froze. The floor of her stomach gave way.

Oh, shit.

Her one-night stand was her fucking boss.

"The new accountant..." Mason's words trailed off as he looked up from his desk and their eyes met.

June's heart stuttered, and she couldn't get any air into her lungs. She rested her palm on the doorjamb, almost feeling faint. He settled back in his chair, his lips curved up in a devilish grin.

A grin she'd only memorized just a few nights ago. He ran a hand along his jawline that still had the scruffy shadow of hair along it. She blinked, remembering how it had felt on her inner thighs. Mason stood from his chair, dressed in jeans, a white button-down shirt, the collar unbuttoned, the sleeves rolled up to reveal his forearms. He strolled around the desk, his hazel eyes locked on her.

"Well, we meet again," he drawled.

June closed her eyes for a brief moment before opening them. She pulled what little strength was left inside her and stood to her full height and entered the room.

"You two have met?" Blair asked with a puzzled look.

"Um, yes. We met the other night at the Little Pint," June said, recovering.

Mason met her halfway and held his hand out for her. She slipped her smaller one into his. It enclosed around her. Those callouses almost snatched a moan from her.

These same hands had slid along her thighs and pushed them open—

She blinked and met his gaze. The glint in his eyes revealed he knew exactly what she was thinking. His gaze dropped down to her lips, and it darkened immediately. She didn't even want to know what he was thinking. She knew what her lips had done. They had fit so perfectly around his—

She snatched her hand back from him.

"She was there with Tanika who introduced us," Mason replied calmly.

He turned back to Blair and smiled. He went over to his desk and leaned back against it. He folded his arms in front of his chest, just looking so relaxed while June was in full panic mode.

"But I didn't know you were who you were," June said quickly. She didn't want him to think that she had been using him.

Well, she had, but not for reasons related to her employment. She'd had certain needs, and this man right here had fulfilled every single one of them and more.

"And I didn't know who you are. I knew Blair had hired someone, but I'll be honest, I hadn't paid attention to the name. Once she said you were qualified, had experience, and she felt you were a fit, that's all I needed to know." Mason shrugged.

"I thank you for having such confidence in me." Blair beamed. She turned back to June. "I'm sure you and Mason will be working closely together. The last accountant we had left a mess. That I can't apologize for."

"It's quite all right. Even if they'd have left stuff in order, I'm sure I would have reorganized things my way." June was trying to stay professional, but how could she? She'd unknowingly slept with her boss. "I'll try not to bother you too much."

"My door is always open to you, Junie B. Whatever you need, just let me know," he said.

That same glint was in his eyes that she'd seen just a few days ago. His gaze did a once-over on her, and her body immediately responded. Her nipples erected into buds, her core clenched, and her heart rate sky-rocketed.

June's face flushed at his use of the nickname he'd given her. She glanced over at Blair who was oblivious to anything.

"Well, I'm glad you two have had the chance to meet. We're going to head back down to her office so I can finish onboarding her." Blair motioned for June to follow her.

She turned on her heel, happy to escape Mason's office. She paused at the door and glanced over her shoulder.

Mason was still watching her. He even had the nerve to toss her a wink. She swallowed hard and shut the door behind her. Blair was already halfway down the hall. She scurried behind the older woman, her thoughts racing.

Was she going to have to quit her new job?

$\maltese$ 4 $\maltese$

It had been a little over a week since the shock of seeing June walk through his office doorway. With all of the craziness going on, he'd trusted Blair to hire the new accountant. Blair had worked for him for years and knew what was needed for the company.

If it's meant to be, maybe we'll run into each other again.

June's words had echoed through his head ever since she'd left. He had assumed that after the night they'd shared, they would have had breakfast, he would have taken her home, and they would have exchanged numbers.

The sounds of her cries of ecstasy still

rang in his head. So did the image of her face as she reached her orgasm. The taste of her had been so damn divine, then to glance up as he'd feasted on her to see her body arched off the bed as she came, had him growing hard right now.

Mason swallowed and stood from his desk. He'd barely been able to get anything done. He walked over to the large windows of his office that overlooked the snow-covered town of Langdale. With as much snow that had fallen this past weekend, June was lucky she hadn't been snowed in with him. Had they been, he would have had plenty of activities for them to occupy themselves.

Each of them would have required them to be naked.

He bit back a curse and tried to reel in his thoughts. He reached down and adjusted his damn cock that suddenly had a mind of its own. He turned away and went back to his desk. There was no way he was going to be getting any work done at the moment. His mind had been too occupied with Junie B.

The woman was avoiding him.

It didn't take a rocket scientist to know

this. So far, when she'd had questions regarding contracts and invoices, she'd just emailed him. Each of her communications had been direct and polite. He'd offered to meet with her, but she'd kindly declined, stating she didn't want to tie up his time while she weeded through the old accountant's records.

It was bullshit.

He bent down and saw another email had come from her about fifteen minutes ago. He clicked on it; she was questioning an unpaid invoice. She informed him the gentleman had said Mason told him he could pay on a payment plan. She needed confirmation of the agreement, since there was no contract showing that.

He thought of the staff meeting where'd he needed to meet with core staff. The entire time she'd avoided meeting his eyes, then raced out of the room as soon as it was over, leaving no chance of them conversing afterward.

He blew out a deep breath. This was getting out of hand. He'd quickly figured out all of this had to do with their night together. He had been as shocked as she had been when Blair had brought her in. They needed to talk. They would eventually need to address the elephant in the room. There was nothing wrong with what had happened between them.

Hell, he wanted her.

He wanted to get to know her. Hear her laugh again. Let her know that he wanted to explore what was between them. He was surprised his house hadn't gone up in flames that night.

An instant message appeared on his screen. It was the office group chat Justina had created for interoffice communication.

> Fresh triple bean was just made.

Justina knew exactly what he needed to hear. The woman was a saint to keep the coffee flowing around this place. He'd run and grab a cup and then come back and try to focus. He had an important conference call with one of his vendors in an hour. He needed to be sharp with the negotiations for this meeting. He was hearing the pricing on materials was going up and he'd be damned if they tried to overcharge him.

This situation with June was far from over.

He collected one of his favorite mugs from the shelving unit behind his desk and headed down to the break room. He was sure everyone would be making their way there. Justina's coffee was famous. She had a secret recipe she refused to share with anyone.

Mason opened the door to the break room and went inside. It was empty aside from the object of his desires standing in front of the microwave. He took a few seconds to study her. Her cream dress tied at the waist, showcasing her curvy frame. Thick stockings covered her legs, and a pair of heels gave him ideas. Her hair was up off her neck in a bun on top of her head. He inhaled sharply, wanting to pull her into his arms and nuzzle her neck with his face. The memory of her perfume came back to him.

She must have sensed someone was in the room with her. She glanced over her shoulder and froze. She didn't say anything but stared at him before turning back to the microwave beeping.

"Mason. Hello." Her soft voice floated across the room. She busied herself with taking her food out of the microwave and heading over to one of the tables.

"You've been avoiding me," he stated. He bit back a grimace. Not the way he wanted to start the conversation they needed to have, but now that it was initiated, he needed them to finish it.

"I don't know what you mean." June glanced over at him with her wide eyes.

The woman was a horrible liar. She knew exactly what he was talking about. He walked across the room over to the coffee machine and lifted the carafe. He poured a hefty amount of the coffee and set the carafe back down. He took a sip of the hot brew which was perfect as always.

He moved over to where she sat and drew out the chair directly across from her. He sat and stared at her. She took her time stirring her food. The aroma from her bowl reached him. Chili, one of his favorite wintertime meals. She was currently adding cheese, those Ritz crackers, and sour cream.

He arched an eyebrow at the amount of cheese. She caught him watching her.

"I like my chili cheesy," she murmured.

"Or do you like a little chili with your cheese?" he asked.

That earned him a smirk from her. He settled back in the chair and watched her take a taste of her meal.

"Are you just going to sit there and watch me eat?" she asked.

"If it will get you to speak with me," he replied. He took another sip of his coffee. He had an hour to kill before he was due on the phone. At this moment, the most important thing was to get this woman to talk with him.

"What is there to talk about? What happened between us, we now know was inappropriate." She shrugged. She sipped her drink and set it down to return to her meal.

"Inappropriate? Why?" he asked.

June paused and stared at him. This had to be the longest she'd looked at him since their night together. Her warm brown eyes were just as he remembered. Her smooth brown skin was radiant, and those lips of hers were plump and full. The images of his cock sliding between them filled his mind. His breath caught in his throat. The woman had known what she was doing. His fingers had entwined in her hair —

"Because I work for you. Had I known last Friday that your real name is Reuben and not Mason—"

"Reuben is my first name. No one called me that except my grandmother who passed away ten years ago. Mason is my middle name. I've gone by that since I was seven years old," he interjected. He didn't want her to think he had misled her in any way. He set his cup down on the table and leaned forward. He wasn't the type of guy who went out and deceived women to sleep with him. Hell, he'd been shocked she'd asked to leave with him.

"It doesn't matter. You are my boss. Plain and simple. Nothing else can happen between us," she said. Her gaze lowered back to her bowl. She gave it another stir. "We should keep everything professional from this day forth."

"And that's it? We just forget what happened between us?" He tilted his head to the side. He honestly couldn't believe she was trying to brush them under the rug. He bit back a grin. She didn't know him, but she was going to find out that he was very stubborn and what he wanted, he would have.

And she was who he wanted.

"There was no us. It was just one night." She sighed, rolled her eyes, and blew out a deep breath.

"But there could be more," he offered.

"Mason—Mr. Reynolds, we can't." She shook her head fiercely.

He grinned at her wide-eyed expression. He actually liked hearing her call him Mr. Reynolds. He'd never been one to be formal about the title of CEO or anything. He encouraged all of his employees to call him by his chosen name—Mason. But right now, the way his last name rolled off her tongue, he wanted to hear her say it again.

"We can. Do you think people would care if there was something going on between us?"

"Yes. I don't want anyone to think the only reason I got this job was because I slept with you." There was fire in her eyes when she looked at him.

He was riling her up and he loved it.

"I'm sure everyone knows Blair hired you and I had no part in you taking this job." He leaned back and folded his arms. He was prepared to argue Junie B down to prove a point. No one would care about them. June didn't have to worry about anyone looking down on her. He actually employed a few couples. She would just have to see Langdale was different than where she was from.

"Still, it's not right. Can we please move on and not mention that night again?" June asked. She was practically pleading with him with her eyes.

"I can't," he murmured.

Her eyes widened. She set her spoon down as he stood. He moved to the chair directly next to her and sat by her. Being this close to her allowed him into her space where her perfume accosted him. He breathed it in and knew he wouldn't be able to get her out of his mind. He reached up and brushed a strand of hair from her eyes. "Junie B, you think I can just forget how you looked taking my cock? Or how you creamed around my finger when I made you come?"

"Mason," she bit out his name around clenched teeth. She glanced over at the door as if someone had magically appeared. "Please don't."

"Or forget how tight you fit around me when I was deep inside you?" He needed to remind her of how good it had been between them. How could she just walk away from that just because she worked for him? He had never, and would never, sleep with an employee, but June didn't count. They hadn't known who each other was that night. He was willing to make an exception.

"Stop it. Someone will hear you."

"Like how I'm sure my neighbors heard you screaming my name?" He arched an eyebrow at her. He let his hand fall away from her. He leaned back and grinned.

At that moment, the door opened, and Justina flew into the room.

"Hey, guys. Tried the coffee?" she asked.

"You made it perfect as always," Mason replied.

Justina walked over to the coffee pot to check it. He snagged his mug and brought it over to him. This conversation with June was far from over. They were just getting started.

"You must have been the first one to come down. I'll come back and check it to see if I need to make some more. Have y'all heard the weather reports? A storm is headed this way," she said.

Mason wasn't shocked to hear about a storm. December was always a heavy snow month for their town.

Justina pushed away from the counter and snatched something up. She headed back to the doorway and grinned. "But first I need to find a place to put this. You know, for the holidays!"

Justina held up a piece of mistletoe then disappeared through the doorway.

June took that opportunity to start packing up her lunch. She pushed up and stood while tossing stuff back into her bag.

"Where are you going?"

She pressed the top onto her bowl before placing it in the bag. "Well, I do have a job to do that you are paying me a very generous salary to do." She zipped up the bag and draped the strap over her shoulder.

He stood and took her hand when she tried to turn away from him. She stiffened and eyed him.

"We aren't done with this conversation, Junie B," he murmured.

"But we are, Mr. Reynolds."

She'd tried to put emphasis on his last name to try to deflect, but all it did was make his damn cock hard. He closed the gap between them and lowered his lips so they brushed against her ear.

"I'm not done with you at all, Junie B. You can run now all you want. I love a good chase."

She snatched her arm from his hold and backed away. Those big brown eyes of hers held him captive till she spun on her heel and practically ran out of the room. He chuckled and snatched up his mug and strolled to the door.

June Young was going to be his.

The weatherman hadn't lied this time. The storm barged in mid-morning, building up all day. It started with a soft flurry of snow, then morphed into a heavy fall by late afternoon. Now, thick snow pressed against the windows. The wind howled something fierce, breaking June's concentration.

She rubbed her eyes and blinked at the blur of numbers on the computer screen. Her desk was a mountain of paperwork that included invoices and payroll reports. All of this had been left for her by the previous bookkeeper. There had been errors in almost every single folder, unchecked balances, and calls that needed to be made first thing in the morning so she could continue to sort out this mess.

A yawn snuck up on her. She stretched her arms above her and settled back in her chair. She glanced over at the time stamp in the corner of her screen and almost fell out of her chair.

Seven o'clock.

She was sure everyone had left by now. Justina had poked her head in at one point when June was deep in reviewing an account.

"Don't stay too long, June," Justina encouraged. "It's getting bad, and a lot of us are leaving early so we don't get stuck here."

"I won't be too much longer," June mumbled, not even looking up from the papers she was studying.

Once she'd finished with that project, she'd wanted to check in on something else, and now it was hours later, she was still here.

Oops.

Now the office was silent except for the hum of the heating system and the whistling of the wind. The glow from her desk lamp was golden against the coldness of the storm outside. She smiled at her favorite lamp she'd brought from home. It was a halogen bulb that burned candle wax to allow her to have soft lighting along with the favorite scent of the candle sitting underneath it.

But when her thoughts should have been on the numbers, they weren't.

They were on him—Mason.

Her boss.

Her mistake—or what she was trying to convince herself, and him, but he wasn't hearing it.

Yesterday in the break room, he'd cornered her with that sensual voice of his, reminding her of all the things that had transpired between them.

The man played dirty.

His words had been on a loop in her head ever since.

Junie B, you think I can just forget how you looked taking my cock?

Like she needed him reminding her. She couldn't forget how he'd felt, or how her body had responded to his. She groaned quietly and pressed her fingertips to her temples. She needed to stop thinking about him and that night.

Mason was her boss. He literally signed

her checks. What happened before needed to remain as buried as she was sure her car was right now.

The lights flickered once. Then twice. Her stomach's bottom gave way.

"You better not," she warned as she stared at the lightbulb of her lamp. The hum of the heater faltered then came back. She glanced at her computer screen that had gone dim.

Was the power truly about to go out? She hoped not. Maybe this was a sign for her to leave now, before the storm got even worse. She began organizing the folders so they would be in order for her to address them when she returned. She froze at the sound of a knock. Her heart pounded. Hadn't everyone left?

The knock sounded again.

"Come in," she called out.

She sat still, waiting to see who was on the other side of the door. The door opened, and Mason's head appeared in the buttery light. He must have been outside. Snowflakes clung to his coat and hair.

"Hey, I didn't think anyone else was here until I saw a second car parked outside." He stepped inside and closed the door behind him. The faint scent of the outdoors and cedar followed him in.

"I could say the same about you. I thought I was the only one here," she murmured. Her pulse galloped like a horse at full speed.

"I was finishing up a few things and didn't realize how bad the snow had got. I thought I could dig my truck out, but it's a lost cause right now."

June frowned and stood. She went over to the window and took in the scene outside. The world was nearly white. The streetlights glowed through the curtain of snow while the cars were half buried.

"Oh, it really is coming down." Maybe she should have left when Justina suggested. She bit her lip and stared at the amount of snow and where her car should be. It looked like a small hill of snow at the moment.

"They are saying the roads are closed. The plows can't keep up. Looks like we're snowed in for a while."

"Here?" June's head snapped around. "You mean we can't leave?"

He gave a low chuckle and came to stand

next to her. His gaze drifted from her to the snow-covered scenery.

"Not unless you want to risk sliding into a ditch then freezing to death. I've got some blankets in my office. We can ride this out there."

Panic filled her. She wasn't afraid of staying in the building with Mason. This was more complicated than that. The thought of being trapped with him appeared to make every nerve in her body come alive.

"Mason, this isn't—"

"What? Don't tell me this isn't appropriate. I'm offering to keep you safe and warm during a snowstorm." He stepped closer to her, enough that she had to tilt her head back to meet his gaze. His hand came up to cup her cheek. "Do you think I would take advantage of you under these types of circumstances?"

"No," she whispered.

They may not know each other well, but she didn't get the sense he was a creep or someone who would force himself on her. Everyone in the office raved about him, as did the customers she'd spoken with.

"I said there would be more between us,

and I meant that, but it would only be if you want it, too."

For a moment, the outside world vanished and it was just the two of them. The howling of the wind calmed down, while the tension in the room grew thick. The lights flickered again, then went out, basking them in darkness.

June's heart slammed against her chest. Automatically, she found herself taking a step toward him. The office was now in complete silence. No heating unit, no electric buzz that one ignored. The only sounds were their breathing and the wind.

"So, um, you have blankets in your office?" she asked.

Looked like they truly didn't have a choice. Mason's hand slipped down and took hers in his.

"Yeah. Grab your things. We'll go up there and wait out the storm."

JUNE WAS CONVINCED THE STORM HAD swallowed Langdale whole. Snowdrifts pressed against the windows in a thick sheet, while the wind continued to howl. Inside Mason's office, it was dim and quiet but warm. The only light came from a few candles he had found in an emergency kit. Their flickering radiance painted the walls in a soft glow and shadows. They created a halo around the sofa where June sat wrapped in a blanket. Mason had arranged the sofa so it faced the open windows so they could watch the storm.

The air smelled faintly of chocolate. Mason stood by a small battery-powered kettle, where steam rose from the spout as he poured hot water into two mugs for their cocoa.

"Do I need to ask why you have that?" A small smile played on her lips, and she watched him prepare their drinks at his desk.

"It was a gift from my mom. She's always worried that I'll starve to death when I get snowed in here."

"So this isn't your first time getting stranded at work during a snowstorm." She shook her head. It would appear the two of them had something in common. Mason was a workaholic just like she was.

"A few times." That crooked grin of his appeared. He straightened and picked up their cups and headed over to the sofa. "But this is the first time I've had company."

He handed her one of the mugs. She took it, and their fingers brushed. A pulse of heat rippled through her. She murmured her thanks and brought the cup to her lips. The drink was warm and delicious. It was definitely something that was needed on such a cold night.

He sat beside her, the couch dipping slightly. They sat in a comfortable silence sipping on their drinks while watching the snow flurries outside the window. The candlelight flickered across his face, catching the faint stubble along his jawline and the curve of his mouth.

June's core clenched. She tore her gaze from him and turned back to the window. She tried to push down the image of him from her mind. Her heart skipped a beat as memories surfaced again. She closed her eyes, the war waging inside her.

On one hand she didn't want anyone to think ill of her for becoming involved with Mason. She was new to the town and the company. She couldn't afford to develop a certain reputation, even though Mason appeared to think no one would care.

But then on the other hand, she was losing a battle at resisting this man. How could she work with him every day and be in a state of arousal from one smile from him, or a smoldering stare thrown her way? Her mind was leading her in one direction while her body was going in the opposite direction.

"You should have gone home earlier," Mason's voice broke through the silence. He turned to her. "Why'd you say?"

June stared into her cup for a moment before answering.

"There's so much to fix. I hate to say it, but the person before me was terrible at their job. Everything is a mess, and I don't want to let the company down. I feel as if this job is really important." She gave a big sigh and shook her head. "I guess I'm a perfectionist, which is good and bad. Ever since..." She trailed off, unsure if she should continue.

"Ever since what?" Mason murmured. There was pure curiosity in his eyes as he watched her. Nothing else. No judgement. Just him waiting for her to continue.

"I became single. I figured I would leave relationships alone and threw myself into my work," she finished. She raised her cup to her lips and took another sip to try to busy herself.

"So the last guy cheated on you with another woman or something?" he asked gently.

A sarcastic laugh fell from her. "He had been cheating on me with two women. At the same time. Somehow, he was able to juggle three of us without me knowing it." She'd never found out if the other women knew of each other or her. She had been hurt and angry when she'd found out. She'd tossed the loser's stuff out in the yard and blocked him. There was no excuse for what he had done to her. Instead of being a man and being honest with her, he'd thought he could have his cake and eat it, too.

"I'm sorry he hurt you."

June's throat constricted. She hadn't meant to open that door, but the words had slipped out before she could stop them.

"Don't worry. It won't happen again," she said.

The wind rattled the windows, and for a heartbeat, she thought they were done with the conversation. Mason set his mug down on the floor and leaned back, resting his arm along the back of the sofa.

"Listen, I am not that guy. I'm not here to hurt you, June. I want to be up front and honest with you."

Her chest ached at the emotions in his voice. Somehow, she knew he was being sincere with her and wasn't trying to run game on her.

Now she felt bad she'd mentioned Corey and his infidelity.

"I shouldn't have brought that up. It's still a bitter pill to swallow." She had thought she'd been in love with Corey. Thought they would be taking the next step and getting engaged. His cheating caused her to reach a low point in her life. Made her feel less than a woman. She'd even questioned why she wasn't good enough to the point where he needed two other women.

So she had thrown herself into her work and figured she would remain single.

"I do want to get to know you, June. I want a chance. We can take it slow. One day at a time," he said.

June's guard began to slip. The tension between them had shifted. It was still electric, but now it was threaded with something deeper.

"You make it sound easy," she said.

They still had the one thing standing between them that he was going to ignore, apparently. She finished off her drink and set the empty cup on the table beside the sofa.

"Maybe it could be. It doesn't have to be difficult if we don't let it."

June stilled and eyed him. She felt the pull between them. It was strong and undeniable. She should get up and create some distance, but instead she found herself leaning closer to him. Her gaze dropped down to his lips.

"June," Mason murmured. "Are you sure about this?"

She didn't answer with any words. She closed the gap and pressed her lips against his. The blanket fell from her shoulders as his hands came up to cradle her face. His thumb caressed her cheek, and he deepened the kiss. The world outside vanished as nothing else mattered but this moment.

When they broke apart, June couldn't tear her gaze away from Mason's. She could no longer fight the pull. She wanted to experience what she had the other night with him. One night was not going to be enough.

June threw caution to the wind. She moved and swung a leg over his lap. Mason helped guide her down to straddle him. His large hands cupped her ass and brought her flush against him. Her fingers threaded themselves into the hair at the base of his neck. They stared at each other, then their lips merged together again.

This kiss was much different than before. This one was laced with passion and heat. Mason's lips and touch flamed the fire that had been left smoldering inside her. His warm hands slid underneath her top, meeting her bare skin. A shiver rippled through her. She tore her lips from his and stared at him. Her breaths were coming in hard, short pants. She reached for the bottom of her shirt and brought it over her head. Goosebumps appeared on her arms once the cool air kissed her skin. Mason leaned forward and blazed a trail of hot kisses along her neck, shoulder, and the center of her chest.

A moan slipped from her. Those lips were needed in more places. She reached behind her and unclasped her bra. The contraption loosened, and she removed it and flung it casually over her shoulder.

"So fucking beautiful." Mason captured one of her mounds with his hands. Her breasts fit perfectly in his palms. He brought her forward and suckled her nipple. The tight little bud disappeared into his mouth.

June's hips rocked forward, dragging her center over the bulge that rested underneath her.

A gasp escaped her. June ached in places she was sure Mason would be able to soothe. She tilted her head back and stared at the ceiling while Mason feasted on her. The sweeping of his tongue over her skin sent a ripple of fire through her. June's skin grew flushed and warm. Her hips moved, teasing the both of them. Mason's eyes locked with hers. The heat in them surged as he gripped her tight to him.

"June," he rasped.

"I want this," she whispered.

Her fingers dropped down to the edge of his sweater. She tugged it over his head and tossed it over her shoulder. They took their time undressing one another as if it were Christmas morning and they were presented the biggest gift. In between heated kisses, their pile of clothing grew until June settled on top of Mason again—this time, naked.

His thick length rested beneath her. She groaned and rubbed herself on him. Her swollen clit dragged along the length of him, sending shivers down her spine. One could argue it was the chill in the air or Mason's cock drawing this response from her.

Their lips were currently molding to one another. Mason's tongue swept inside June's mouth while his hands held her steady in place. He tore his mouth from hers, leaving hot wet kisses along her jawline.

"Lift up," he urged.

June rested her hands on his shoulders and did as he'd commanded. He reached between them and positioned the broad head of his member to her slick opening.

"Yes," she hissed.

June was desperate to feel Mason breach her. The memory of the way he filled her drove her to slide down on his length. She ignored the slight twinge of pain. Her muscles stretched to accommodate him. She paused and had to take in a deep breath.

"That's it, Junie B. Breathe, baby," Mason said softly.

June held his gaze as she took another breath, settling down completely on him until he was fully submerged into her tight channel. The world disappeared around them. She no longer cared that Mother Nature was waging a war on their small town. It was just the two of them. Mason's warm chest crushed to hers as he lifted her, bringing her down on him. The possessive hold he had on her left no doubt that he was going to ensure they both remembered this night.

The intensity in his gaze did something to her. He held her still while his hips thrust upward, sending his cock to unbelievable depths. She cried out, holding on to him while he filled her to capacity. In this moment, she felt...alive.

Wanted.

June wrapped her arms around Mason. His name fell from her lips in a chant, and he continued to pound inside her. Heat pooled low in her belly, sensations racing through her. With each of his thrusts, her swollen little bud was rubbed from the movements. Her breath was coming in pants. She had a hard time catching her breath. Mason's lips were on her skin; he surrounded her, filled her...gave her everything she'd ever wanted in a lover.

He slammed her down on him repeatedly, almost unmercifully. June's cries filled the air. She held on for dear life, but soon her orgasm was racing toward her. It forged into her like a runaway train. A scream erupted from her as she reached her peak.

"Fuck!" The word tore from her with each wave of her release washing through her.

Mason's hips quickened until he, too, released a roar. Her body shook along with his. A warmth filled her; his seed flooded her. Mason's grip on her was bruising, but she didn't offer any complaints. He continued to fill her. June fell forward onto his chest. He held her to him, their bodies glistening with a fine sheen of sweat. Both of them were spent and out of breath. June had no words for what she'd just experienced.

Instead of saying anything, she just allowed Mason to hold her. She didn't want to move at all. His semi-soft cock was still buried inside her, and that alone was a good reason not to move. He must have felt the same. He reached over for the blanket and covered them. She glanced up and caught him staring at her.

"It's going to be all right, Junie B. I promise," he murmured. He pressed a kiss to her forehead and tucked her head into the crook of his neck.

She breathed in his tantalizing scent and decided to just take it one day at a time.

June steered carefully down the slushy road. Her wipers squeaked against the windshield, fighting off the stubborn snowflakes that continued to fall. Christmas music drifted through the speakers, but she wasn't truly in the mood for hearing about Santa and his many reindeers.

Not when her thoughts kept circling back to him.

Two days had passed since the storm and she'd broken her rule. She couldn't keep the memory out of her head of Mason's touch, the warmth of his breath sweeping along her skin, or the way he'd looked at her in the afterglow of their snowed-in activities.

It had felt like it meant something.

And that could not be the case.

He'd been the perfect gentleman after-ward. No awkward morning-after silence, no cocky grin that said I told you so.

Instead, he'd made them coffee, cleared a space by the window so she could watch the snowplows work. He'd even followed her home to ensure she arrived there safely. He hadn't asked for anything. Just offered her a warm smile and a "see you Friday."

Now she was completely confused. She wanted to see that smile. She hadn't wanted to wait for Friday. He'd given everyone the day off after the storm due to the amount of snow that had fallen.

Her phone buzzed against the console. She hit the hands-free button once she saw who it was.

"Good morning," she answered.

"Is it? Doesn't sound like it." Tanika chuckled. "Have you not had your coffee yet?"

June grumbled to herself. She should have swung by the Java Hut and got her something to help start her day. But since she didn't know how the roads were, she'd decided to forgo coffee for safety.

"It's just..." June paused. She wasn't sure if she wanted to spill the beans on what had happened the other night. This was her best friend, but she still hadn't forgiven her for not telling her who Mason was at the bar. Of course Tanika had been shocked that she hadn't known. She had thought they had met when she'd interviewed.

"What? Is something wrong?" Tanika's bright voice suddenly lowered with concern.

June sighed, and her shoulders dropped. She might as well tell her.

"It happened again," June mumbled. She tightened her grip on the steering wheel, the tires slipping slightly. Ice was hidden beneath the slush on the road. She should have stayed home and worked remotely, but seeing how she was the newbie with a mountain of work to get through, she'd opted to go on into the office.

"What happened— Oh, wait! Are you telling me you slept with Mason again?" Tanika whispered loudly. She fell into a fit of giggles. "Never mind. By the sound of your voice, I know you did! Tell me everything."

"Nothing to tell. We were snowed in, there was hot cocoa, candles—"

"And you let him bang you like a Christmas drum!" Tanika howled with laughter.

June brought her car to a stop at a red light. She pinched the bridge of her nose while Tanika laughed at her expense.

"That's my girl!"

"Tanika," June breathed heavily.

"I'm sorry, babe. It's just funny to me how you were so against getting involved with him that you went ahead and did the thing you said you wouldn't do—again," Tanika said. She cleared her throat and got herself under control. "What are you truly worried about?"

"This thing between us," June admitted.

"Well, it's not like you can unkiss your boss or take back the sex. You might as well see where this goes. What's the harm?"

"Well, people finding out for one. Two, I don't want to get hurt again. You know what Corey did," June said. The light turned green. She gently pushed down on the gas to get her car going again.

Tanika had been right there to help her get through those dark days. She didn't know what she would have done without her. Having a true friend had been lifesaving at that time.

"Listen. We all have to protect our hearts, but you can't lock yours away forever. Mason is not Corey."

June bit her lip. The snowflakes swirled past the windshield. She took in the snow-covered town and found it to be a beautiful wonderland.

"You are supposed to tell me I'm crazy," June murmured. Was she going to consider taking Mason up on his offer? One day at a time. They could slowly get to know each other, but what if they just kept it a secret from the office? Then if things didn't work out, no one would know.

"That would only come out of my mouth if you were to call me and tell me you were getting back with Corey." Tanika snorted.

"That will never happen," June said dryly.

"Well, I wasn't calling for anything, but if something else happens with the boss again, you better call me ASAP. I'll keep the popcorn ready."

The call ended with Tanika's laughter

echoing in June's ears, and even June found herself smiling despite her worry.

As the town's Christmas decorations came into view—wreaths hanging on every lamppost, the giant pine twinkling in the town's center—she couldn't shake the knot of nerves forming in her stomach. She had figured she would stay single for a while, and the thought of starting a new relationship downright scared her.

❧

THE OFFICE SMELLED OF PINE AND cinnamon, thanks to the candles Justina had left burning at the front desk. June slipped off her coat and forced a steady breath, then headed to her office.

No one knows you and Mason had sex here. Calm down.

She tried to force her racing heart to slow down, but the pounding muscle had a mind of its own.

Just focus on work. Invoices. Payroll. Not him.

Except that was going to be impossible. Memories of that night surfaced, her body temperature rising. She swallowed hard and scurried on to her office. She slipped inside and hung her coat up on the hook behind the door. She turned around and froze. On her desk was a paper cup from the Java Hut. Steam curled from the lid, and something was written in black ink across the side.

Morning, Junie B. Thought you could use an extra shot—M.

Her heart skipped a beat while her lips curled up before she could stop them. The handwriting was neat, firm. Masculine. Just what she would expect from Mason. She sat and stared at the note. Took her first sip. It was warm and perfect. How did the man know how she liked her coffee?

She couldn't contain the grin that overcame her. She reached over and turned her computer on and enjoyed her coffee while waiting for the computer to start. By midmorning, she'd buried herself in spreadsheets and ignored the fluttering in her stomach every time she heard his voice. She was halfway through reconciling a few invoices when she received a direct message from Justina.

> There's a delivery guy at the front desk with a package for you.

June stretched and figured she'd just go down and grab it. She'd been at her desk all day and needed to take a breather for a moment.

> Be right there.

She pushed back from her desk and stood. Her aching muscles revealed she was well passed her break. She quickly headed to the front desk. Justina must have stepped away. A tall, dark-haired man with a crooked grin and dimples for days waited for her. Several boxes sat on the desk in front of him.

"I have an overnight delivery for Miss June Young," he said.

"That's me." She walked around to the front of the desk and took the tablet he handed her. She quickly signed her name.

He leaned against the counter and studied her. "So, Miss June Young is working through the holidays, huh? Someone's dedicated."

"Or just swamped." She chuckled and handed him back the tablet.

"Do you need help carrying these boxes?" His grin widened.

"She's got help," a familiar voice cut in. Mason stepped into the lobby. His tone was polite, but there was an edge to it. He casually walked forward with his hands in his pockets. "Is there anything else you need?"

"Um, no, sir. I was just dropping these off." The delivery guy stood to his full height.

"Appreciate it." Mason nodded.

The guy gave June another smile before spinning on his heel and heading out the door. She waited until he was gone before she turned to Mason.

"What was that?"

"This is the paperwork from Danbury Farms?" he asked.

She stood staring at him as he ignored her question. "It is, but you didn't have to—"

"I didn't like the way he was looking at you," Mason said softly.

He stood next to her but kept a little distance between them. It didn't keep her from breathing in his familiar cologne or seeing how the light reflected in his eyes.

"Mason," she sighed.

"I know. We're at work. I'll behave." He lifted a hand, a faint smile tugging at his lips. He set a small candy cane down on the desk before her. "For being good."

"You are impossible." Her cheeks warmed at the gesture.

She snatched the candy cane up while he picked up the two boxes. So the man knew how she took her coffee and knew how addicted she was to peppermints around this time of year.

Who was feeding him this info?

"Oh, good. You got the delivery. Sorry, I had to pee like crazy. I guess all that coffee got the best of me." Justina breezed back into the lobby with a wide smile. She took her spot behind the desk at her computer and answered the phone just as it rang.

"Yes, thank you," June said. She folded her arms in front of her as if needing to hide the candy cane from Justina.

She and Mason left the lobby and continued on.

"Maybe I am impossible," he murmured, continuing their conversation now they were out of earshot of anyone. He eyed her as they walked to her office. "But I think you like me that way."

Her face warmed even more. The man just didn't know how much she liked him. She tried not to stare at him but couldn't help it. Her gaze dropped down to his perfectly muscular chest that was hidden underneath his casual button-down shirt, and the jeans that molded him perfectly. She snatched her eyes away and kept them straight ahead. She had basically memorized what this man looked like naked, and right now was not the time to be remembering. They went into her office where he placed the two boxes on her desk.

"You know I could have carried them," she said.

A glint appeared in his eyes. He pressed close to her and leaned down so his lips brushed her ear. The warmth of his breath sent a shiver down her spine.

"I'm well aware of what you are capable

of." He gently nipped her ear before he backed away from her.

Her mouth fell open as she watched the man turn and disappear from her office. Her knees grew weak in that moment. She went and took a seat in her chair and placed the candy cane on her desk and stared at it. It was ridiculous to think that something so small could make her heart race, but then she realized it wasn't the piece of candy.

It was the giver of the gift.

Maybe Tanika was right. She couldn't unkiss her boss. Maybe she didn't even want to.

❧   7   ❧

The Stone & Willow Tavern was alive. With the festive decorations and holiday decor that promised Christmas magic, it was buzzing with laughter, conversations, and holiday music. Every year, Mason hosted a Christmas Eve party for the entire company. It was his way of showing appreciation to every member of the team. It also allowed the different departments to come together to socialize and relax. But at the moment, Mason could not relax. He was tense, scanning the crowd looking for her.

Then he saw her.

June.

She stood near the corner by the fireplace. Her hair caught the soft lamplight, her coat draped over one arm. She laughed at something Chuck, one of the field guys, said. She was absolutely radiant with the way her eyes crinkled with amusement. His chest tightened. He didn't like the fact another was standing so close to her or making her laugh.

It should be him.

"Who's the woman you're staring at?" Hunter, his younger brother, appeared beside him.

His attention was on the pair as well. Hunter worked out in the field as a foreman. Mason trusted him to run the projects.

"That's June. She's the new bookkeeper." Mason's jaw flexed as June laughed at something else Chuck said.

"Oh, okay. I think I've gotten an email or two from her. Nice to put a face with the name." Hunter folded his arms and glanced back over at Mason. "So why are you staring daggers at Chuck?"

Mason blinked and tore his attention from June and Chuck. "What are you talking about?"

"You look as if you're ready to go over

there and drag Chuck away from her. Something going on between you two?" A smirk appeared on Hunter's lips.

At the moment, Mason didn't feel like trying to explain the situation to him. Plus, there were too many people around. June wanted to keep things hush-hush about them, but he was finding it damn hard.

"That is none of your business." Mason slapped Hunter on the shoulder and headed through the crowd. Hunter's laughter followed behind him. He noticed the subtle ways the other men paid attention to her. Not in a disrespectful way, but enough that he had a familiar emotion appear in his chest. Possessiveness.

Unable to resist any longer, he walked toward her. She excused herself and made her way toward the double doors that led to the deck. He arrived at her side just before she opened the door.

"Going outside?" he asked.

"Oh!" June jumped slightly. Her brown-eyed gaze landed on him. "Um, yeah. I wanted to get some fresh air."

"It's a little cold out there." He helped her put her coat on. Her hat hung slightly out of her pocket. He snagged it and slid it onto her head. "There."

"Mason. You didn't have to do that." A small smile appeared on her lips.

His heart skipped a beat at the expression in her eyes. He'd seen it before when they were snuggled up on the couch in his office.

She tugged her coat tighter around her. "Enjoying the party?"

"I am now." He pushed open the door and ushered her outside. The door closed behind them, and they walked over to the banister of the deck. "Finally. I get you to myself."

Her eyes flicked to the tavern windows behind them where the party continued on with its holiday cheer.

"You've been waiting to get me alone?" she asked.

"Yeah. I didn't think you'd appreciate it if I'd taken you away from Chuck." He hid his hands in his jeans pockets to keep from reaching for her. He had forgone a coat and wore a thick wool sweater.

"I mean, as long as you wouldn't have been a caveman, it would have been all right. I was hoping to get a chance to see you tonight." She turned away and glanced at the sky.

It was a beautiful night with the crisp air surrounding them. Mason ignored the temperature. He was completely focused on the woman beside him.

"I wouldn't want to give anyone any ideas about us," he admitted. He wanted to honor her request. As much as he wanted to let the entire world know they were together, he would keep them a secret.

"Mason, what if this doesn't work out between us? Then what? Have you thought about that?" Her voice was low, and she continued to stare off into the distance.

"No, I haven't thought that far ahead," he said. And he didn't want to. There were these feelings swirling around inside him that he would admit he'd never felt before. He didn't know if this was love or what, but he knew he wanted her.

Needed her.

"Well, I have. I just wouldn't want that embarrassment or that awkwardness between us if we were to split. Then I'd probably have to look for another job."

"How are you already figuring we won't work out? You're barely giving us a chance." He almost reached for her, but he had to resist. He glanced back over at the doors. No one from the party was paying them any attention. The music seemed to have gotten louder, as did the laughter and conversations. "Let me take you on an official date."

She studied him for a moment. She chewed on her bottom lip and pondered his request. His gaze dropped down to that lip, and he ached to replace her teeth with his lips. His breath caught in his throat at the memory of her kisses.

No longer able to resist, he took one of her hands in his.

"Please." He entwined their fingers together and gave her a little squeeze.

"I guess we should get to know each other besides, you know, the other way to get to know one another." She giggled and leaned into him. Her features softened as she gazed up at him. "What do you have in mind?"

"How about dinner and ice skating?" Each winter the town constructed an ice rink for the locals. Everyone took advantage the fun outing.

"I haven't been ice skating since I was a kid," she said bashfully.

"That's okay, I used to play hockey. I can teach you a thing or two," he said. He was thrilled she was willing to take this first step. He wanted to show her how serious he was about her. She was beautiful, intelligent, and this thing between them was worth investigating.

And if things didn't work out between them, he'd ensure it wasn't awkward. Someone with her skills with numbers was a bonus for his company. He'd be an idiot to let an employee like her go. In her short while on the job, he'd seen a difference.

"Well, then consider it a date," June said. Her gaze drifted down to their linked hands then back to him. Uncertainty and longing warred in her gaze. The wind blew gently, lifting a few strands of her hair from underneath her hat.

Mason inhaled, savoring the moment. She shivered, and he motioned for them to go back inside. He guided her to the door and rested a palm on the handle.

"Tomorrow?" he asked.

"You do know tomorrow is Christmas, right?" She arched an eyebrow at him.

"Do you have plans?" He was already coming up with a few date ideas for them. Was she going to visit her family? He was sure his mom and dad would be expecting him to show up for dinner. Was it too soon to introduce June to them?

"I had planned to go over to Tanika's parents' house for dinner. I'm going to go home to visit mine next weekend for the New Year," she said. She shivered again and leaned into him with a small teasing glint in her eyes. "But I can make time for you."

"Good." He opened the door and ushered her inside to get her out of the cold.

A faint murmur of cheers rose as they paused in the doorway. All eyes were on them. Justina pushed her way through the throng of people and pointed above their heads. Mason glanced up and froze.

A sprig of mistletoe dangled above them.

Mason's lips twitched into a smile.

"Oh." June's eyes widened. She stared at the mistletoe. She flicked her gaze to him. She began shaking her head.

"They would eventually find out," he whispered.

The fight left her eyes; gently, he brought her close to him and pressed a chaste kiss to her lips. It lingered just long enough to set his heart racing.

The room exploded in laughter and more cheers.

"It's about time!" Justina shouted.

June laughed and pulled back just enough that he could see how bright her eyes sparkled. Mason held on to her, glad that his point had been proven. He leaned down and kissed her again.

"I told you so," he said against her mouth.

She rolled her eyes and tapped him on his chest with her hand. "You've been waiting for this moment, haven't you?"

"To let everyone know that you're with me? Yes." He wasn't ashamed to admit that he wanted everyone know June was his woman.

She glanced around and took in all of the playful grins and bets being called in for payment.

"Wait? Were they taking bets on us?"

She gasped. It was obvious Justina had led the betting ring amongst the other employees.

"Apparently." Mason chuckled. He glanced at her and brought her into the tavern farther away from the door. It was getting late, and he had rented out the place until closing time. There was still plenty of food and drinks for everyone. "Want to get out of here?"

She eyed him for a moment. "What do you have in mind?"

"Whatever you want to do?"

She chewed on her lip again and eyed him. She blew out a deep breath and smiled.

"I guess it wouldn't hurt if we left together. It looks like everyone already knows about us." She spun around and led them through the establishment.

A few people stopped them along the way for small chats before they arrived at the exit. A light snow had begun to fall. They left the building and stood on the sidewalk. June turned to him and smiled.

"Your place or mine?"

June stirred awake to the soft hum of holiday music drifting through her home. The smell of coffee wrapped around her like a warm hug and forced her to open her eyes. She blinked and glanced over at the sunlight spilling in through the windows. It was then she remembered, she wasn't alone.

Mason had stayed the night.

She sat up and stretched then swung her legs over the edge of the bed. She gripped the sheet around her, the coolness of the air tickling her naked skin. She smiled, feeling that familiar soreness between her legs. Her bladder decided to alert her that she needed to hurry and take care of business. She grumbled slightly and stood. She released the sheet and padded over to her closet and snagged her robe. She made her way into the bathroom to answer nature's call. Before leaving the bathroom, she took a few moments to make herself decent since she had company.

She tightened the ties on her robe and headed out of her bedroom to find Mason. He stood at the kitchen counter, her apron tied around his waist, flipping pancakes and humming along with the music. Her heart swelled at the sight. The chaos, the stress, the snowstorm, the office—it all seemed miles away now.

Now, in its place was this.

A normalcy.

She and her man on Christmas morning.

"Morning." Mason glanced over his shoulder with a warm grin that weakened her knees.

"Good morning," June whispered.

He set the spatula down and motioned to her. She went to him. She drank in his bare chest, jeans that rode low on his waist, and bare feet. Somehow, he made cooking breakfast the hottest thing in the world.

His warm arms closed around her in a strong hug. She tipped her head back to meet his gaze, but his lips covered hers before she could blink. The man certainly knew how to greet a woman in the morning. The kiss was gentle but held the promise of more to come. He lifted his head and smiled down at her.

"Coffee?" he asked. He kissed her lips.

"Please." After the night they'd had, she was going to need a little pick-me-up.

The man had been insatiable, but then so had she. He turned and opened her cabinet as if he lived there. He pulled a mug out and poured her a cup. He even had the audacity to know where everything was to doctor up her drink the way she liked. He handed her the mug.

"Thank you."

She inhaled deeply. The rich, comforting aroma greeted her along with something else. Was that cinnamon? Or maybe just the scent of him, tucked into the folds of her memory now mingling with the present.

"I hope you're hungry." He went back to the stove and slid the pancakes onto a waiting plate.

"You made breakfast?" she asked, moving to his side. She took in all of what he'd prepared. How long had he been up?

"Yeah. I figured after last night, we deserved a proper start to our Christmas."

"You are amazing." A laugh escaped her. She shook her head. "But I'm not complaining."

It was nice to have a man cook for her. She couldn't remember Corey ever boiling water for her. She sighed and took a sip of her perfect coffee.

"Good. We can eat." He motioned over to the island where she had a couple of chairs.

She took her seat and waited patiently as he plated up their food. Her eyes widened at the portions he served her when he set her plate in front other. She held back a chuckle, knowing she wasn't going to eat it all, but she wasn't going to say anything. Apparently, her man wanted her to eat good on Christmas morning.

Her man?

Might as well stop fighting this.

Yes, her man.

They ate in a comfortable silence. She

kept stealing glances at him as if expecting him to disappear. Was this man even real? The way he pursued her, was patient with her, made her toes practically curl any time he touched her, now he showed that he could cook, too?

She almost wanted to pinch herself.

Once they were done, they tidied up the kitchen together before taking fresh cups of coffee into the living room. She had a small tree in the corner that she and Tanika had decorated one night while drinking plenty of wine. Mason must have turned the lights on. She had a few presents tucked underneath it.

She took a seat on the couch near the large window. She loved having it positioned there because it allowed her to look out on her street. Mother Nature had been hard at work again last night. There was so much snow. Her street looked like a winter wonderland after the addition of a few inches.

June's eyebrows rose as she watched Mason head over to the tree and snag a small gift that she hadn't noticed.

"What is that?" she asked.

He came to sit beside her. He placed his

mug on the side table and took hers from her to place it next to his. He handed her the beautifully wrapped gift. The paper showcased a jolly Santa and a smiling snowman on it.

"It's for you." He reached up and brushed a stray strand of hair from her face.

"Mason…" She hesitated. Her fingers brushed over the smiling snowman. Her heart stuttered slightly. She looked over at Mason. Now she felt bad. She didn't have a gift for him.

"Open it," he encouraged, his gaze steady and warm.

June bit her lip and carefully removed the paper. Inside the box was a delicate snowman figurine, a note tucked beneath it.

Our First Christmas.

June's throat tightened while tears blurred her vision. She traced the snowman with her fingers, her heart swelling in ways she hadn't thought possible.

"It's beautiful and perfect," she whispered.

He pulled her into a gentle hug and rested his chin on the top of her head.

"I'm glad you like it." He dropped a kiss

on her head, then chuckled. "Not sure what I would have done with it had you shot me down."

She barked a laugh and slapped him playfully on his chest. Their smiles faded when he lowered his head. He took her lips in a deep, sensual kiss, reminding her of the fire that burned between them. She melted against him, getting lost in the kiss.

She allowed herself to believe that maybe she could love again.

Love the right person, that was.

She eased back slightly and rested her head on his chest, embracing the warmth of him against her.

"Will you go with me to my parents'? I know you said you had plans with Tanika, but I would love for you to meet my family." There was a hesitancy in his eyes as he watched her.

She sighed and loved how the man wasn't afraid to show his vulnerability with her. She smiled and nodded. She was going to throw caution to the wind and go with the flow.

"Sure. Maybe we can still swing by Tanika's parents' home? I have a few gifts to hand out there," she said.

The way his face lit up let her know she'd made the right decision. This man was special, and she'd be a fool to let him go.

"Of course." He pressed a kiss to her lips again. He leaned away and had a sheepish look on his face. "Can I say that this so far has been the best Christmas?"

"Because it's our first Christmas together," she said softly.

He brushed her hair from her face again and kissed her again.

The snow began to fall once more. June let herself sink fully into the moment. Mason took the figurine from her and placed it securely on the table before lifting her onto his lap. Her fingers dropped to the ties of her robe and opened it. Her core clenched at the heat that flared in his gaze.

"Merry Christmas, Mason." The robe dropped down onto the floor, forgotten.

He tore his attention from her breasts and met her gaze.

"Merry Christmas, Junie B." He reached for her and took her lips in a hard kiss.

A moan slipped from her, and she

wrapped her arms around his neck, bringing their bodies flush with one another.

As she turned her pleasure over to Mason, a fluttering thought passed through her mind.

The best gifts aren't found under the tree— they're the ones you find when you take a chance.

And Mason was the best gift this holiday.

All because of a dare.

EPILOGUE

Mason watched the first light of morning spill over the Smoky Mountains, golden and soft, painting the peaks like a promise of good things to come. The cabin was quiet, the air crisp, and for the first time in months, he just savored the moment.

June stepped out onto the deck with her coffee in hand. His chest tightened at the sight of her. She was breathtaking even in her robe with a sleepy look to her. The way she moved toward him left him feeling nothing but love for her. He could watch her and never get tired of it.

He'd whisked her away for a break from Langdale and the constant pull of work. She had been working long hours, and in the short time since she'd joined the company, she had turned it around. He decided to take them on vacation because she deserved it. She rarely took time off work or did anything for herself.

But in reality, he wanted her alone, because he realized that he couldn't wait any longer for this moment. He was in love with June.

Deeply, irrevocably, hopelessly in love with her.

She was everything he would ever want in a woman. Beautiful, intelligent, funny, and she had a big heart.

"Morning." He leaned against the banister of the deck and held his arm open for her. He loved how she automatically floated to him and sidled up next to him. They fit perfectly together in every way. Her curvy frame pressed close to him. He dropped a casual kiss to the top of her head.

"Good morning," she said.

Mason's heart stuttered. She smiled at him and, like always, he felt unraveled from one glance from her. He pulled a small velvet box from his sweatpants pocket and held it out to her.

"I have something for you," he murmured.

Her hand went to the box. She hesitated before taking it. She paused and glanced back at him.

"Mason..." she whispered. Her big brown eyes grew wide as she looked back at the box.

He knelt before her, feeling that this was right. With every breath he took, he knew he needed her to be there with him forever.

"Six months ago, Tanika dared you to go home with me," he began.

"She told you?" Her voice ended in a shriek. She rolled her eyes and muttered something about her friend that sounded like a death threat. "Oh my God."

"Well, I'm glad you took her up on the dare. One night turned into me wanting to spend every day with you. Every morning, I wake up and realize I want more. Mornings like this and the ones we have when we spend the night together back in Langdale. I want more of you. I want all of you."

June's chest rose and fell rapidly. Tears

teetered on the edge of her eyelids as she watched him.

"Mason," she breathed. She blinked, and the first tear fell, blazing a trail down her brown cheek.

"Now I'm issuing a dare." He took the box back from her and opened it, revealing the delicate ring that sparkled even in the muted dawn light. "For you to spend the rest of your life with me."

June set her mug down on the ledge and wiped the tears from her face.

"Yes." Her voice broke, but she still nodded. "Yes, Mason. Of course I will."

Relief filled him. He slipped the ring onto her finger. He stood and brought her into his arms. He kissed her gently at first and savored the moment. June was going to be his wife. His future. The kiss deepened, and he began to picture their future together.

"I love you," she murmured against his lips. Laughter bubbled through her tears. She sniffed and combed her fingers through his hair.

"I love you more," he replied.

He rested his forehead on hers and inhaled deeply. She laughed and pressed her body to his. He lifted her slightly and spun them around. She wrapped her legs around him and held on, squealing. He walked over to the door of the cabin and went inside, still carrying her. June's legs and arms tightened around him, sending a wave of desire through him, and it went straight to his cock. She nestled her face in the crook of his neck. Her warm breath caused chills to ripple down his pine.

"Come on." He had thoughts of taking her back to their bedroom, but the couch was closer. He dropped her onto it and pulled his shirt over his head. "Our forever starts right now."

His woman opened her robe to reveal she was naked underneath it. June's lips curved up into her sexy little grin. She turned and spread her legs wide. His gaze locked on her slick center, her swollen clit peeking out as if looking for him.

"I'm ready for forever," she whispered.

Mason dropped to his knees before her, thankful to have this woman who would become his wife. He drew her hips to the edge of the couch so he could enjoy his early morning feast.

A NOTE FROM THE AUTHOR

Dear reader,

Thank you for reading The Christmas Dare. I absolutely love coming back to Langdale each year. These stories are too good not to share with my readers.

I hope you enjoyed Mason and June's story! This was a fun story to write! These winters storms in Langdale are no joke!

We will continue to get more stories in this series. Don't you worry!

If you love this series, please tell your friends about it and don't forget to leave a review on the platform you purchased the book!

Happy reading,
    Peyton Banks

A LANGDALE CHRISTMAS

Holidays are never the same when a winter storm blows in...

Heat up your holidays with these unforgettable stories—because in Langdale, love is the greatest gift of all. Get ready for unputdownable stories that will leave you yearning for more. The snow may be falling, but the temperature is rising in Langdale. Are you ready to unwrap the gift of love during Christmas?

If you love small town romances during the holidays, then you will enjoy A Langdale Christmas series.

Start this series today!

SURGEON BOOK BOYFRIEND

BOOK BOYFRIEND DATING AGENCY

Kimora Tucker had one dream in life: to help people. As one of the top lead researchers at her hospital, her dream was becoming a reality. She didn't anticipate that one of the physicians whose patients were enrolled in her study would create roadblocks in her groundbreaking work. He reminded her of one of the heroes in her favorite romance novels—arrogant and hot.

Needing a distraction from the stresses of work, Kimora downloaded the Book Boyfriend Dating Agency app in hopes of having fun. If she could get paired up with the perfect fantasy book boyfriend, why not?

Only her match was him. The one person she never expected to find on a dating app, let alone be matched with. It was a twist she never saw coming.

They say Book Boyfriends are our consolation for men in real life. What if we told you that meeting your fantasy hunk is just a click away?...

Tag Along for a series of sweet & spicy encounters between empowered women and the BBFs who fall for them!

USA TODAY bestselling author, Peyton Banks, is the alter ego of a city girl who is a romantic at heart. Her mornings consist of coffee and daydreaming up the next steamy romance book ideas. She loves spinning romantic tales of hot alpha males and the women they love. Make sure you check her out!

Sign up for Peyton's Newsletter to find out the latest releases, giveaways and news by scanning the QR Code.

Want to know the latest about Peyton Banks? Follow her online:

- tiktok.com/@peytonbanks_author
- facebook.com/peytonbanksauthor
- goodreads.com/peytonbanks
- bookbub.com/profile/peyton-banks
- instagram.com/peytonbanks_author
- bsky.app/profile/authorpeytonbanks.bsky.social
- threads.com/@peytonbanks_author

ALSO BY PEYTON BANKS

<u>Current Free Short Story</u>

Summer Escape

<u>A Langdale Christmas</u>

The Christmas Secret

The Christmas Wish

The Christmas Gift

The Christmas Wonder

The Christmas Dare

<u>Silver Creek Ranch (Shared World)</u>

Wrangling Her Cowboy

Falling For Her Cowboy

<u>Lunchtime Chronicles (Peyton's)</u>

Polish Boy

Thick & Beefy

Rich & Decadent

<u>The Keith Brothers</u>

Mr. Hotness

Mr. Arrogant

<u>Blazing Eagle Ranch Series</u>

Back in the Saddle

Knockin' the Boots

Roping a Cowboy

Country at Heart

Cowboy, Take Me Away

Hard to Forget

Lasso My Heart

<u>Special Weapons & Tactics Series</u>

Dirty Tactics (Special Weapons & Tactics 1)

Dirty Ballistics (Special Weapons & Tactics 2)

Dirty Operations (Special Weapons & Tactics 3)

Dirty Alliance (Special Weapons & Tactics 4)

Dirty Justice (Special Weapons & Tactics 5)

Dirty Trust (Special Weapons & Tactics 6)

Dirty Secrets (Special Weapons & Tactics 7)

Dirty Ultimatum (Special Weapons & Tactics 8)

<u>SWAT boxset, books 1-3</u>

<u>SWAT boxset, books 4-6</u>

<u>Trust & Honor Series (BWWM)</u>

Dallas

Dalton

<u>Interracial Romances (BWWM)</u>

Pieces of Me

Hard Love

Retain Me

Silent Deception

Surgeon Book Boyfriend

<u>African American Romance</u>

Breaking The Rules

<u>Mafia Romance</u>

Unexpected Allies (The Tokhan Bratva 1)

9 798993 210865